D1074798

Jodie's Shabbat Surprise

For my family who makes Shabbat special, and for my mother
who taught me how it is done. – A.L.

To my amazing daughters, who always stand by me, both as family
and as the most truthful reviewers of my work. – K.T.

KAR-BEN PUBLISHING
A division of Lerner Publishing Group, Inc.
241 First Avenue North
Minneapolis, MN 55401 USA
1-800-4-Karben

For reading levels and more information, look up this title at www.karben.com

Main body text set in Spitz Com Book 13/21.
Typeface provided by Linotype AG.

Library of Congress Cataloging-in-Publication Data

Levine, Anna (Anna Yaphe)
      Jodie's Shabbat surprise / by Anna Levine ; illustrated by Ksenia Topaz.
         pages   cm.
      Summary: During their Shabbat walk in the park, Jodie and her dog Digger find the perfect
birthday present for her archaeologist father.
      ISBN 978-1-4677-3465-3 (lib. bdg. : alk. paper)
      [1. Sabbath–Fiction. 2. Dogs–Fiction. 3. Gifts–Fiction. 4. Archaeology–Fiction. 5. Jews–
Fiction.] I. Topaz, Ksenia, illustrator. II. Title.
PZ7.L57823Jq 2015
[E]–dc23   2014003602

Manufactured in the United States of America
1 - PC - 7/15/14

Jodie's Shabbat Surprise

BY ANNA LEVINE

ILLUSTRATED BY KSENIA TOPAZ

KAR-BEN
PUBLISHING

Jodie dreamed of being a famous archaeologist just like her dad. She wanted to uncover treasures hidden deep inside the earth. She was sure her dog Digger did, too.

"Find Dad's slippers," said Jodie.

Digger barked and ran off.

"No Digger.
Not Dad's lucky hat."

"Find Eli's baseball," she tried again.

Digger came back with her brother's
smelly baseball socks.

"You'll never be a famous archaeologist with Digger as your helper," said Eli.
"He's hopeless."

"And he needs a walk," said her mom.
Digger brought Jodie his leash.

"Be home in time for Shabbat. And while you're out, try to think of something new we can get for your father's birthday next week."

Jodie and Digger headed over to Porcupine Park.
Friday afternoons the park was full of walkers and bikers.

Taking off Digger's leash, Jodie let him run free while she sat in her favorite spot to think. She wanted to find the perfect gift for her dad but she couldn't think of anything. A new hat? He liked his old one. A new flashlight? But his favorite one still worked.

"Diiiiigger!" Jodie called. "Time to go home. Where are you?"

It was getting close to Shabbat. Bikers were getting on their bikes. Walkers were heading home. Even the wind had stopped. It became quiet. Everyone was going home to where it was safe and warm and smelled of freshly baked challah and the promise of a tasty Shabbat dinner. Suddenly Jodie felt alone.

Just then Jodie heard a yelp. Digger? She parted the shrubs beside her and saw a hole in the ground.

She poked her head inside. "Over here,
Digger." She shimmied her shoulders farther
in. Closer, but not close enough. She wiggled
in her waist. Her thighs. Her knees. Until
more of her was in than out.

"I almost have you, Diiiiigg . . ."

Tumbling, turning, somersaulting, Jodie fell into the rock-lined pit and landed with a kerplunk.

"Ouch!" she said.

Digger jumped up and gave her a big wet kiss.

"Fortunately, famous archaeologists never go anywhere without their flashlights," thought Jodie, "because it looks like there's something here besides dirt. Too bad we didn't bring our tools."

Digger grabbed the toe of Jodie's shoe and tugged. "Of course!" Jodie pulled off her shoe and took off her sock. "We can use my sock to brush away the dirt without ruining the surface. Good thinking, partner.

"Wow! Look at these stones and the shape of the hole. I can't wait to ask Dad what this is all about."

The next day, after Shabbat lunch, Digger, Jodie, and Dad went for a walk in the park. Jodie showed him the hole.

"What a find, Jodie!" said her father. "This is a wine press.

"Back in the days of the Bible the pickers would squish the grapes by stomping on them. The juice would run over the stones, leaving behind the seeds and pulp. Then it flowed into the pool where it was collected and put into jars."

"The grape pickers stomped on the grapes with their bare feet?" asked Jodie.

"I'm sure they first washed their feet," said Dad with a chuckle. "Imagine what fun this must have been."

"Digger," Jodie whispered, when her father was far enough away. "I think I have an idea for Dad's birthday."

The next day she called her father's friend David, who was also an archaeologist.

He told her what needed to be done to clean out the wine press.

Jodie and her friends carried out buckets of dirt.

They swept the ground.

Then she told her
mother her plan.

The morning of Dad's birthday, David invited him to the park. "I hear you and Jodie found something interesting. I'd like to see it." As the two archaeologists walked through the woods, past Jodie's favorite sitting spot, they heard the sounds of yelps and howls and laughter.

"Surprise!" yelled Jodie and the crowd of people behind her.

Jodie's mother had brought enough grapes to fill the wine press to the top. Jodie and her friends had taken off their shoes, washed their feet, and rolled up their pants.

Everyone was stomping and squishing and squashing the grapes so that the juice
flowed over the stones into the pool. Soon there was enough juice to fill a bottle.

"Happy Birthday!" said Jodie, who was covered in purple stains, with purple pulp in her hair and purple juice between her toes. "We didn't buy you something new for your birthday, because the best present you can give an archaeologist is something very, very old!"

Mom and Jodie poured glasses of juice for everyone.

"Sweet and delicious," said Dad. "Our ancestors had the right idea."

Then they all sang "Happy Birthday" and Jodie gave her father a big purple birthday kiss.

Author's Note

Jodie's Shabbat Surprise is based on a true story about the first dog in history to uncover a major archaeological site. One day, Tzach, a puppy in Israel, was out for his walk in Jerusalem's Ramot Forest with his owner, Shaul Yona. Tzach was happily scampering about when suddenly he fell into a hole. Yona rescued him. Something about the hole made Yona curious. He called in archaeologists, who discovered that it had been used as a grape pressing area during the First Temple period. Further excavations revealed additional pits, pottery pieces and bronze coins from the Second Temple period.

After hearing about Tzach, the archaeological pup, I put on my hiking boots, grabbed my sunhat, pocketed my flashlight, just like Jodie, and set out to explore the dig at Ramot Forest for this story. Riki Yona, the Israel Antiquities Authority, the Municipality of Jerusalem, Jerusalem Parks and the Ramot Community Center, have developed the Ramot Park into an archeological site. They invite all of Jodie's friends and readers to come and explore!

About the Author and Illustrator

Anna Levine is the author of two previous "Jodie" adventure stories, as well as two young adult novels which take place in Israel and reflect her experiences of living on a kibbutz on the northern border with Lebanon. Her short stories, poems and non-fiction articles have appeared in Spider, Cricket and Cicada magazines. Anna lives with her husband and two children in Mevesseret Tzion, a suburb of Jerusalem.

Ksenia Topaz was born in Moscow and moved to Israel in 1991. A graduate of Moscow's Strogonoff Academy of Art, Ksenia comes from a family of artists and sculptors. She has illustrated more than 20 children's books. The mother of two daughters, Ksenia lives in Jerusalem.